To
James
Merry Christmas
- 2005 -
Michael J. McFelland

D0503152

Santa's New Job

Much like Santa in this story, I could not do this job alone. I want to thank my wife, Cher, who decorated our house for Christmas in August. Andrea, who brings the story to life with her wonderful paintings. My son David, who photographed my grandchildren in the various settings for Andrea to paint. My entire family, who has been behind this project and encouraged me at all times.

Michael James McLelland

To Grandma and Grandpa Cope for all the wonderful memories, and my baby, Kaden, may you always treasure the spirit of Christmas.

Thank you Grandpa Cope for modeling as Santa Claus and posing in zero degree temperatures for pictures. Also, a great thanks to the author for giving me this fantastic opportunity.

Andrea Cope Kirk

Text Copyright © 2004 Michael McLelland
Illustrations Copyright © 2004 Andrea Cope Kirk

All rights reserved.

No part of this book may be reproduced in any from whatsoever, whether by graphic, visual, electronic, film, microfilm, tape recording, or any other means, without prior written permission of the author, except in the case of brief passages embodied in critical reviews and articles.

ISBN   1-55517-821-9

Published by Cedar Fort Inc.
www.cedarfort.com

Distributed by:

Book design and layout by Design Publishing and Media Group Inc.
Creative Director Seth Taylor
Graphic Designer Brandon Jeppson
www.designpubgroup.com

Printed in the United States of America
10 9 8 7 6 5 4 3 2 1

Printed on acid-free paper
Font Berkeley

Library of Congress Control number
TXU1-148-032

Santa's New Job
By Michael James McLelland
Paintings By Andrea Cope Kirk

The boy on his knee had just turned eight.

"What I really want is a shoe that turns into a skate."

"Give me, give me, give me," was all the boy could say.

Santa thought, *I don't have room in the sleigh.*

I need a new job; I can't do this any longer.

This new idea kept getting stronger.

What would I do if I just quit today?

It might be nice to have a real job, one with real pay.

Andrea C. Kirk

 could be a doctor, a chemist,

Or maybe a cop.

A pilot, a designer, or open a shop.

s Santa dreamed about new jobs,

The future looked brighter, no shopping mobs.

He stood up and stretched and started to leave,

When a small lad tugged and pulled on his sleeve.

"Oh, Santa, please, Santa, let me give you my list!"

The boy thrust forward the note in his fist.

Oh no, not another one, I have made up my mind,

But something in the boy's eyes looked sweet and seemed kind.

So Santa sat for just one more plea.

He lifted the boy up onto his knee.

The list was long, but what a surprise!

As the boy spoke, Santa looked in his eyes.

y dad needs a job, my mom a new coat,

My brother's lost in a place remote,

My sister is sick, they say she could die."

The boy's voice was soft. Santa heard him sigh.

"I feel all alone and don't know what to do.

So I decided to come to see you."

Santa was shocked—such words from a boy.

The list was long but no request for a toy.

**S**anta decided right then and right there,
This was too much burden for a boy to bear.
The problem was Santa couldn't do it alone;
So he got out his list and picked up the phone.
"Hi, Bob, this is Santa, I have a job I need quick—
A sure cure for a sister who is very sick."

hy, Santa, just tell me what to do.

I wouldn't be a doctor if it weren't for you.

I am sure you remember when I was a boy,

The chemistry set, much better than a toy.

I'll do my best, help in any way.

I'll get started immediately; I'm on it today."

T he next call was to John, who had become a cop.

"I need a detective to work non-stop.

Find me a job for a good family man.

Find a brother too, to finish my plan."

"Oh, Santa," John said with a sob.

"A toy gun and badge helped me want this job.

How did you know the perfect gift?

It came at a time when I needed a lift."

Santa smiled as he remembered the day.

A smile on a boy was better than pay.

ext, Santa called a pilot with a plane.

"I have a tough job, if you will let me explain."

"Don't worry Santa, I'll do what you want me to do.

I wouldn't be a pilot if it weren't for you.

It was you that helped me want to fly.

I was young and very shy.

A toy plane, along with a book.

Doesn't sound like much, but that was all it took."

anta's last call was to Sally to sew a new coat.

She had new fabric that had come by boat.

"Oh, Santa, if it weren't for you, I wouldn't know how to sew.

Remember you gave me my machine wrapped up in a bow."

Santa smiled again as he remembered that day.

All Sally did was sew and sew, never stopping to play.

You know, I think maybe this work isn't bad.

I love giving gifts to boys, to girls, to mom, and to dad.

What was I thinking? I have work to do.

Christmas is near for me and for you."

That was Santa's very best year—

The season he learned to hold his job dear.

He worked harder than ever as he did his job.

Of course, his favorite gifts were the ones he gave Rob,

The name of the boy who taught Santa true joy.

Rob's sister got well, and his brother came home.

Dad got a job. Mom, a coat and a comb.

This was a great day. Santa wished he could stay.

W hen Santa got up, it was time to leave.

But for Rob something more was up Santa's sleeve.

"I have something better than a toy, for such a special boy.

Take this gift before I go

Here's a puppy; help him grow."

ld Santa was grinning as he climbed in his sleigh.

"I love my job, and I love the pay."